·中英双语·

猎鲨记

大师插图经典

〔英〕刘易斯·卡罗尔 著
〔芬〕托芙·扬松 绘
李珊珊 译

人民文学出版社

© Text by Lewis Carroll
Illustrations by Tove Jansson © Moomin Characters Ltd./The Estate of Tove Jansson
Original title: The Hunting of the Snark first published in 1876. First publication of the illustrations in 1959 by Bonniers (Stockholm, Sweden).
Published by arrangement with Bonnier Rights Finland, Helsinki.

图书在版编目（CIP）数据

猎鲨记/(英)刘易斯·卡罗尔著;(芬)托芙·扬松绘;李珊珊译.—北京：人民文学出版社，2017
（大师插图经典）
ISBN 978-7-02-013450-2

Ⅰ.①猎… Ⅱ.①刘… ②托… ③李… Ⅲ.①叙事诗－英国－现代 Ⅳ.①I561.25

中国版本图书馆CIP数据核字(2017)第253637号

责任编辑　甘　慧　尚　飞
装帧设计　李　佳

出版发行　人民文学出版社
社　　址　北京市朝内大街166号
邮政编码　100705
网　　址　http://www.rw-cn.com
印　　刷　上海利丰雅高印刷有限公司
经　　销　全国新华书店等

字　　数　40千字
开　　本　890毫米×1240毫米 1/32
印　　张　3.75
插　　页　4
版　　次　2018年10月北京第1版
印　　次　2018年10月第1次印刷

书　　号　978-7-02-013450-2
定　　价　42.00元

如有印装质量问题，请与本社图书销售中心调换。电话：01065233595

目 录

引言 1

第一幕
登陆 1

第二幕
贝尔曼的演讲 9

第三幕
贝克的故事 17

第四幕
捕猎行动 23

第五幕
海狸的教训 31

第六幕
律师的梦想 41

第七幕
班克的命运 49

第八幕
消失 55

CONTENTS

PREFACE 63

FIT THE FIRST
The Landing 67

FIT THE SECOND
The Bellman's Speech 73

FIT THE THIRD
The Baker's Tale 79

FIT THE FOURTH
The Hunting 85

FIT THE FIFTH
The Beaver's Lesson 91

FIT THE SIXTH
The Barrister's Dream 99

FIT THE SEVENTH
The Banker's Fate 105

FIT THE EIGHTH
The Vanishing 109

引 言

　　如果事事皆有可能,那么在这篇短小但充满教育意义的诗歌中,作者也曾被控诉满纸胡言乱语。这样的控诉,我肯定是从"船首斜桅有时候会跟船舵缠绕在一起"(第二幕)这一行开始的。

　　这种可能性难免会让人心生苦闷,但我也不会(当然我也可能会)征引我的其他作品来批驳这一事实:我将不会(当然我可能也会)指出这些诗歌本身存在的强烈的道德目的,指出其在测算时是如何谨慎地遵照算术法则,或者指出其在博物学中的崇高教义——我只是会更多地使用平淡无奇的简单说明来解释这个故事是怎么发生的。

　　贝尔曼对外貌有着近乎病态的敏感和关注,经常一周一两次地将船首斜桅卸下重新上漆,这种事发生得太过频繁,以至于到了时间需要更换它的时候,那船上没有人能记起它应该被放在船舶的哪端。他们知道就这件事儿向贝尔曼抗议是丝毫没有用的——因为每每此刻他都要搬出他的《海军法规》，而且要庄重地读出大家都听不懂的细则——所以这件事情往往都是以贝尔曼更加牢固地稳居总舵主的地位为结局。舵手经常满含热泪地站在贝尔曼身边，即便他知道贝尔曼的航行原则是错误的，但那又能怎样呢？《海军法规》的第42条写明："任何人都不许同站在驾驶舵盘前的人讲话。"贝尔曼自己也被那句"站在驾驶舵盘前的人也不准同任何人讲话"所洗脑，他完全掌控着这艘船。所以，任何的抗议和规劝都是不可能的，而且直到下一个上漆日来临之前，基本上他们也无法进行任何航行。在这段令人困惑的时间里，他们的船通常都是倒退着航行的。

因为这部诗歌作品在某种程度上是与不同层面的废话（Jabberwock）相关的，正好让我借此机会回答一下长期以来被大家问起的一个问题，如何发"slithy"这个音，在单词"slithy"中字母"i"是长音，就像在"翻滚，扭动（writhe）"这个词中一样；还有，"toves"这个词的发音是为了跟"小树林，果园（groves）"这个词押韵的。再次，单词"borogoves"中的第一个"o"的发音跟"借（borrow）"中的"o"发音很像。我听说有人试图将"worry"一词中的"o"发音。这种情况大概就是人类的任性乖张之表现吧。

这也恰巧是一个合适的契机，能让我们来关注一下诗歌中其他的辛苦创作。"矮胖理论"的两种含义被缩写成一个类似的混合词，这对我来说，似乎更能切准文意。

比如，拿"冒烟（fuming）"和"喧闹的（furious）"这两个词来说。当你拿定主意要说出两个词，但纠结于先说哪个好，现在张开嘴巴开始说。如果你的思想更倾向于"冒烟（fuming）"，那说出来的将是"冒烟"，然后再是"喧闹的（fuming-furious）"；如果情况相反，思想只是一丁点地倾向于"喧闹的（furious）"，你可能就会先说出"喧闹的"，然后再是"冒烟（furious-fuming）"；但如果你别具天赋，想要对这两个词"不偏不倚"，那你就会说出"frumious"①。

假如存在上述情况，当皮斯托尔说出那句著名的"臣服于哪个国王？混蛋，要么说，要么去死！"，朱思迪斯·夏洛对到底是臣服于理查德还是威廉姆难以权衡，以至他不能在外人面前说出其中的任何一个名字——这点尚存疑，其实于相比于死亡，他只需脱口说出一句"理查德廉姆！"，就能解决问题。

---

① Frumious，这里是"furious"和"fuming"的合成词。

第一幕

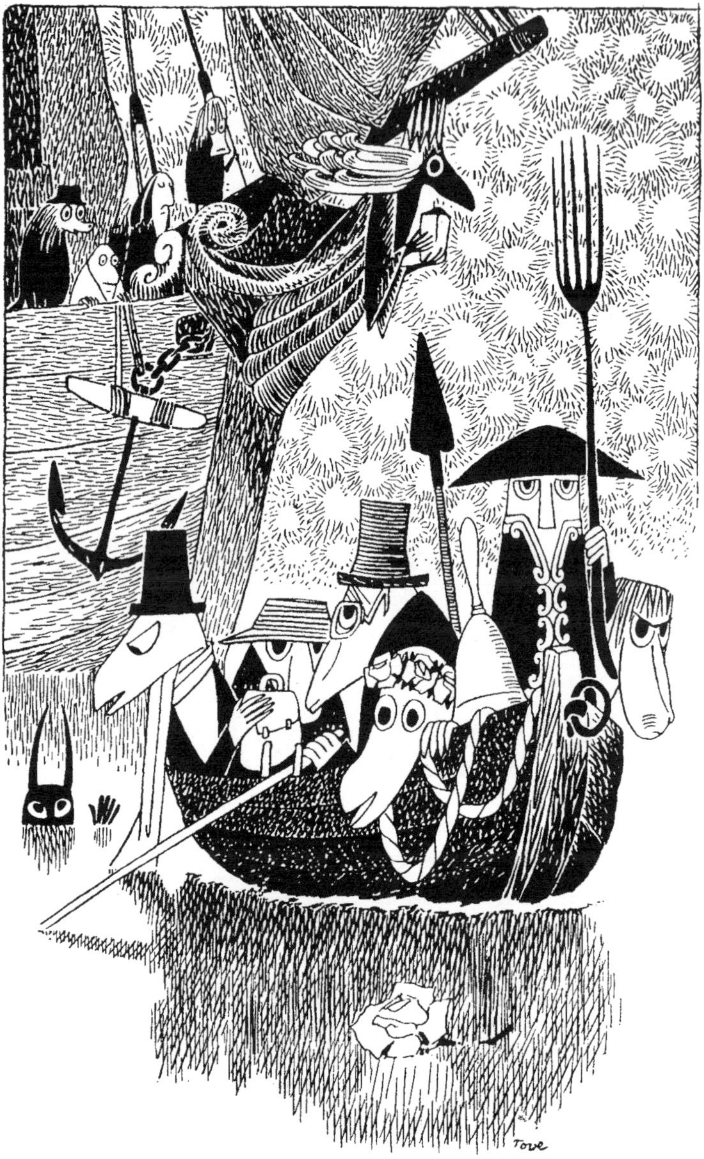
Tove

登陆

"捕猎蛇鲨的好去处啊!"
贝尔曼站在船头,
伸出毛发缠结的手
小心翼翼搀扶着队友
依次登岸。

"捕猎蛇鲨的好去处啊!
重申一遍,
为了给你们加油打气
捕猎蛇鲨的好去处啊!
我已经讲了三遍了:
任何我说三遍的事情都是真的。"

全体船员已经就位:
帽子和头套制造商——布茨;
负责化解纠纷的律师,
为商品估价的布洛克。

保镖比亚德,能力令人惊
赢得的比赛,多得数不清。
财务小班克,掌管金与银
团队管账人,没他可不行。

甲板上来回踱步的海狸,
有时也会坐在船头绣蕾丝花边:
贝尔曼常说,救人他最在行,
没有哪个水手再能比得上。

另有一位,实在健忘,
自打登船,
雨伞、手表、珠宝和戒指,
甚至旅行的衣服,都能忘光光。

四十二个精心打包过的箱子,
每个上面都粉刷了他姓名:
装船时他竟未提及此事
箱子全都留在了海滩上。

损失的衣服无关紧要,因为
他登船时穿了七件外套,带了三双靴子——

但是最糟糕的是,

他竟完全忘记了自己的名字。

对于别人的大叫声

类似"开除我吧!"或是"拉下我的假发!"

或者别人的问话

类似"嗯,你在说什么?"或者"嗯,他叫啥名字?"

他总是喜欢用一句"你好"来回应。

当然啦,他最爱的一句是:

"这事,呃,是一个玩笑。"

对于那些喜欢给别人取外号的人来说,

他的名字五花八门:

他亲密的朋友称他为"蜡烛头",

他的敌人称他为"烤焦的奶酪"。

"从外形上看,他笨拙不堪——智力低下——"

(贝尔曼很喜欢就此调侃嘲笑他。)

"但是他勇气可嘉!而且,毕竟,

这是猎捕蛇鲨最重要且必备的品质。"

他曾经跟土狼开玩笑,

互相摇头晃脑地怒视对方。
又和大熊手牵手散步,
"这么做只是为自己打气,"他说道。

他——贝克——原本作为面包师登船:
被雇佣之后,全体船员苦不堪言
可怜的贝尔曼几近被逼疯——因为——
原来——他只会烘烤婚礼蛋糕——
然而,船上没有任何可以做婚礼蛋糕的材料。

最后一名船员需要被特殊介绍一番,
尽管看起来像一个不可思议的傻瓜:
但是,他满心满脑只有一个念头——"蛇鲨",
善良的贝尔曼几乎是在第一时间就雇佣了他。

他原本作为屠夫登船,
但是,船行一周之后
他严肃地宣布
自己也就只能杀死海狸而已,
贝尔曼恐惧至极,
吓得几乎讲不出话来。

但最终贝尔曼还是颤巍巍地说道,
船上只有一只海狸;
而且那只海狸还是自己拥有过的最温驯的一只
如果它死了,他一定会痛心不已。

海狸,偶然听到这番言论,
噙满泪水抗议起来,
即便是捕获蛇鲨的喜悦
也难以抵消当时那种令人阴郁低落的惊讶。

其他船员,义正辞严地进言:
应该让屠夫单独待在一条小船;
但是,贝尔曼毅然决然地宣称,
只要他还指挥着这次航行,
以上那条进言将永远不会被采纳。

虽然只有一条船、一个铃
领航依然是一门很复杂、很艰难的艺术,
贝尔曼感到恐惧,但为了坚守原则,
更是为了不偏不倚,
他必须婉拒上述提议。

毫无疑问,海狸从这件事中得到的教训就是——
迅速找来了一件二手的——防护大衣。
班克也建议说,下一步要写张官方告示
它才能把命保住。

告示上就写:
这是班克的主意,雇佣或出售
两名优秀的好警员,一个做消防
另一个救危于冰险。

然而,令人胆战心惊的那天过后,
无论何时,只要屠夫经过,
海狸总是警觉地盯着他,
表现出不可言说的畏惧。

第二幕

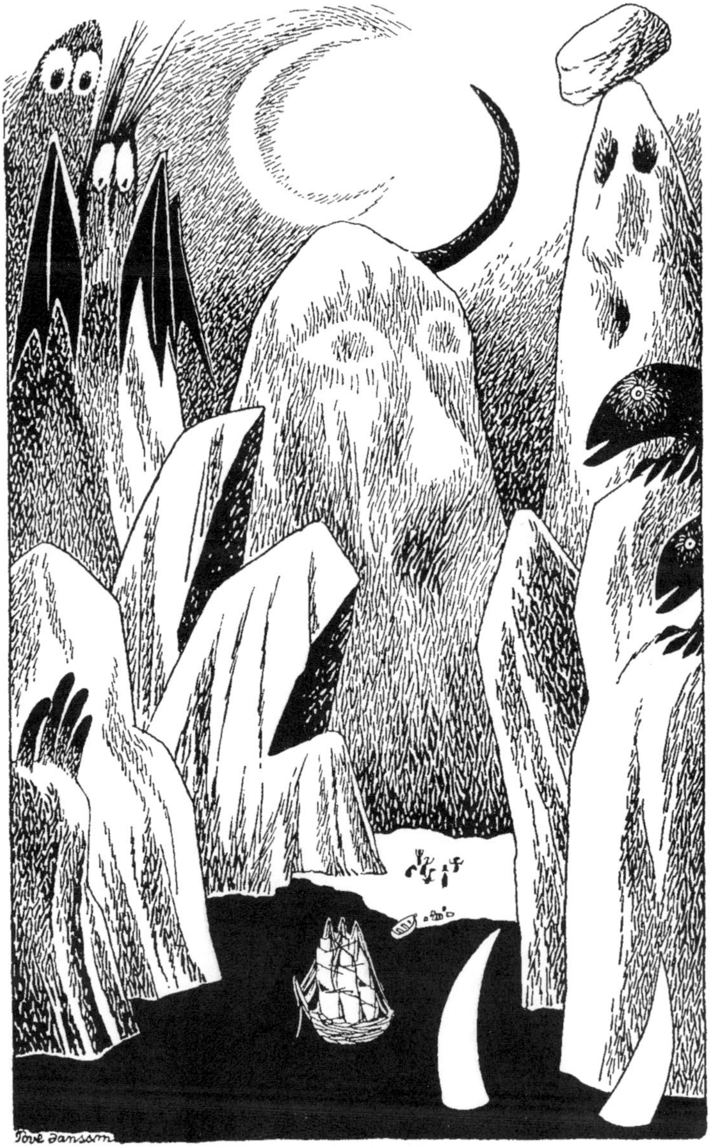
Tove Jansson

贝尔曼的演讲

他们把贝尔曼捧上了天——
如此的旅程,如此的舒缓、惬意!
当然,也是如此的肃穆!
贝尔曼的脸上写满了聪明睿智!

他买了一张巨幅航海地图,
上面是一望无际的大海,
未有半点陆地的痕迹:
船员们开心异常,
因为终于有张地图
能让他们所有人都看得懂了。

每当贝尔曼大声提问:
墨卡托北极点、赤道、热带地区、寒带和子午线的用处是什么?
全体船员就会回答说:
"它们仅仅是一些通用符号!"

"通常的地图
分布着岛屿、峡谷

形状鲜明,
但是要感谢我们英勇的船长。"
（船员们带着抗议嘲讽道）
"他给我们买了最好的地图——
一张完美的、绝对空白的地图。"

显然,这些使航行最初看起来非常迷人；
但是很快他们就发现
他们全心全意信任着的船长
其漂洋过海只有一个目的
就是为了鸣响自己的铃。

船长总是思虑周全,勇敢无畏——但是他所下达的指令
通常会令船员们感到手足无措。
当他大喊："向右转舵,但保持船头还是在左舷上！"
这到底是让舵手怎么做啊?

这样的情况总是会导致有时候船首斜桅跟船舵缠绕在一起：
就像贝尔曼经常会强调的一样,
在热带气候中,这种事情总是频繁发生,
打个比方,有时这艘船就像是被蛇鲨"吞噬"了一样。

但在航行之中，船长也难免失算
这个总是令贝尔曼感到特别的困惑和沮丧
如他曾经希望的那样，当刮起正东风的时候，
这只船就不会往正西方偏航了！

然而危险总会过去——
他们最后还是靠岸了，
带着数目庞大的箱子和袋子：
乍一看上去，眼前的景象不尽如人意，
因为满眼尽是沟壑纵横、峡谷峭壁。

觉察到船员们的士气消沉，
贝尔曼开始以一种类似唱歌的语调
重复他那讲了一个季节、已经烂掉的玩笑——
然而除了呻吟、抱怨声，大伙儿并没有做出其他的回应。

他亲手给船员们盛烈酒，
并命令他们一字排开坐下：
船员们一脸不情愿地坐在那里注视着亢奋的船长，
任由他独自情绪昂扬地做着自己伟大的演讲。

"朋友们,同胞们,请听我说两句!"
(以上来自于他喜欢的语录。
人们为他的健康举杯庆祝,
当他再次将额外的食物分配给大家时,
人们又为他三声欢呼。)

"航行已历时数月,很多周,
(你可能会说四周不就是一个月吗?)
但还远远不够(这些都是船长的原话)
因为我们甚至都还没有瞥到一眼蛇鲨!

"航行已历时数周,很多天,
(你可能会说七天不就是一周吗),
但是我们一直渴望见到的蛇鲨,
直到现在都未能看到!"

"听我说,兄弟们,我再重申一遍
请谨记这五个明确的标记:
一旦记住了这些,无论你们去哪儿,
它们都能确保你一眼识别出真正的蛇鲨。

"接下来让我一一道来,
第一就是体型,
蛇鲨很瘦,身体中段凹陷,线条感很强:
就像穿了件腰部有些紧的外套,
同时还夹带着一丝类似幽灵的诡异气息。

"第二点正如你们所知,
蛇鲨'起床'很晚
这种'晚'已经到了极致,
它总是在每天五点吃早饭,
第二天才吃正餐。

"第三点就是它的反应迟缓、木讷、忧郁。
如果你们谁巧遇蛇鲨并想冒险靠近它的话
你会听到深深的叹息声,仿佛它正处于极度的哀伤之中:
用俏皮话来讲,它看起来表情总是很凝重。

"第四个特点就是
它们很爱干净,
坚信自己是道风景,
可怎么也没人信。

"第五个特点是野心。

特类区分要辨明:

区分那些拥有羽毛,会咬人的种类

以及那些有腮须,会抓伤生物的群体。

"普遍来讲,蛇鲨完全不具有攻击性,

然而,我觉得还是有义务指出,

它们中还是存在一些骇人的怪物——"

紧接着贝尔曼的演讲在慌乱中戛然而止,

因为我们的贝克晕厥了。

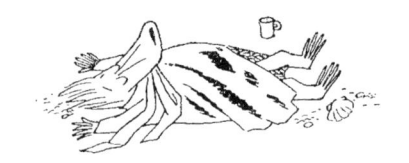

第三幕

Tove Jansson

贝克的故事

（贝克晕厥以后）
大家尝试着用松饼去唤醒他——
用冰去唤醒他——
用白芥末和水芹叶去唤醒他——
用果酱和其他很多法子去唤醒他——
比如，找了很多谜题让他去猜

终于，他能够站起来说话了，
很平静地说要讲一个悲伤的故事；
贝尔曼喝令："保持安静！不要出声！"
同时很兴奋地摇了摇手中的铃铛。

之后气氛陷入死寂一般的沉默！鸦雀无声。
当这个他们称之为"霍！"的男人
用一种不合时宜的声调
讲述他悲伤的故事时，
整条船安静得甚至连呻吟声都听不到。

"我的父母尽管很穷,但都是诚实正直的人——"

"跳过这些零七八碎的开场!"贝尔曼急躁地喊道。

"一旦天黑了,就又没机会捕猎了——

时间一分钟都不能浪费!"

"我跳过了四十年,"贝克满含热泪地说道,

"我甚至没有做更进一步的阐述

就直接跳到了被带上船

帮你们捕猎蛇鲨的那天。"

"当我与亲爱的舅舅道别时,

他说道——"

"噢,跳过你亲爱的舅舅!"

贝尔曼再次一边生气地摇铃,

一边不耐烦地重申道。

"他对我意味深长地说道,"这个温和的男人继续说着,

"'如果你的蛇鲨是一只真正的蛇鲨,那还好:

全力以赴捉住它——烹制好之后与蔬菜一起端上桌,

这是手到擒来的事情。

设下陷阱,不停寻找
千百努力,不停找寻,
高举猎叉,满怀希望,
据其痕迹,索其性命。'"

("就是这个法子。"
贝尔曼迫不及待地插话道,
"这个就是过去别人经常向我提起的
抓捕蛇鲨时应该尝试的方法!")

"'但是,我亲爱的外甥,当天你一定要小心,
如果你遇到的蛇鲨是一只可怕的怪物!
记住一定要消无声息且迅疾离开、消失,
再也不要跟它正面相遇!'"

"就是这个故事,这个我一直铭记在心的故事,
每当想起舅舅最后的这段话,
我的心就像一个注满了颤动的凝胶乳的碗一样
久久不能平静!"

"就是这个,就是这个——"

"我们以前就遇到过!"
贝尔曼愤怒地说道。
贝克也回复道:"我再重申一遍。
就是这个,这个就是我最惧怕的!

"我一直积极投入地猎捕蛇鲨——在每个深夜——
我总是在恍惚中梦到激烈的场面:
我在朦胧中看到自己把它与蔬菜一起端上桌,
这一切看起来都是如此轻而易举。

"但是如果真到了我遇见那只可怕怪物的那天,
我肯定会在瞬间(在我确认的那个瞬间),
就消无声息地迅速逃离——
别说真有那天,我甚至连有这样的念头不能忍受!"

第四幕

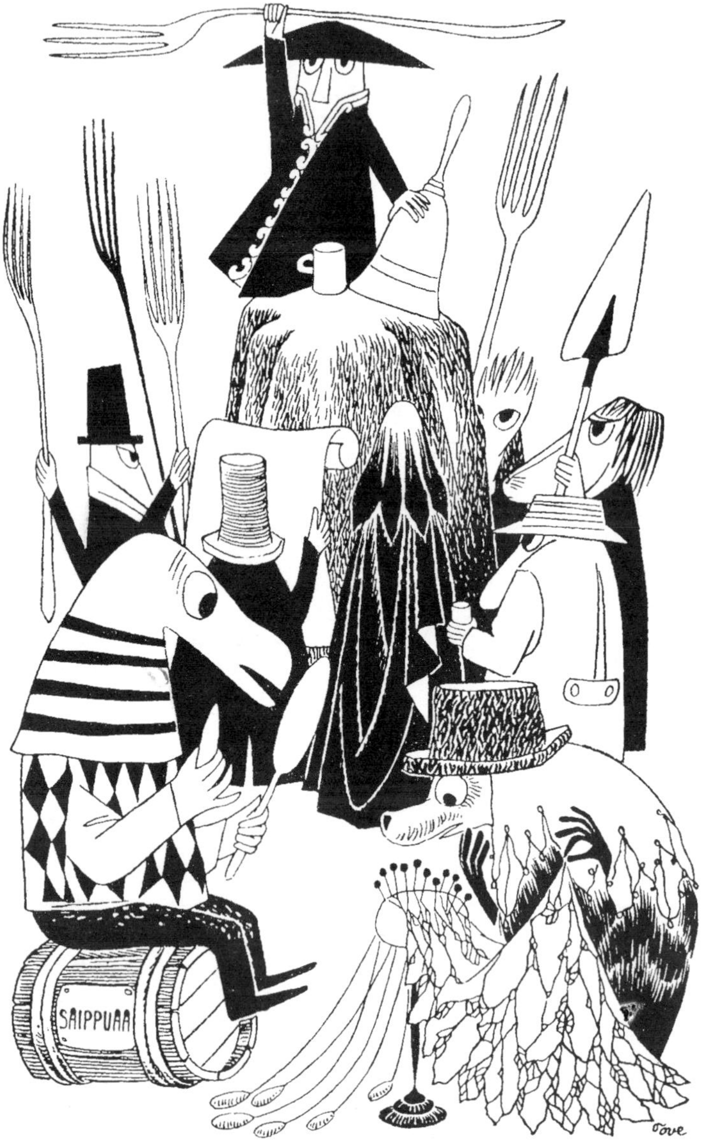
SAIPPUAA
Tove

捕猎行动

听完贝克的话,贝尔曼陷入阴郁,眉头紧锁。说道:
"如果是过去你说这些,无可厚非。
但是现在提起来就显得过分尴尬了,
因为蛇鲨已经在我们'家门口'了呢!

"这样我们的情况就糟糕了
正如你坚持的那样——永远不想再碰它——
如果蛇鲨真如你所说的那么可怕
那么,亲爱的朋友,
你早在航行之初就应该告知,不是吗?"

"现在再提及此事确实会显得更尴尬——
我想这一点我已经都申明过了。"
这个被称为"嗨!"的男人长叹一声,说道,
"在你们上船的时候,我就提醒过你们。

"你们可以控告我谋杀——说我冷漠——
(我们所有人难免都有脆弱的时候)

但我所有的罪行中，
都不会存在欺骗。

"我记得我用希伯来语讲过这件事——用荷兰语讲过——
用德语讲过，用希腊语也讲过。
但是我完全忘记了（对此我万分苦恼）
英语才是你们的语言！"

"一个令人伤感的故事，"贝尔曼说，
脸色也开始越来越难看。
"但现在的你们，已经洞悉自身的处境，
那么再多的争论都只会显得荒诞可笑。

"接下来我要说的话，"他向大家伙解释道，
"平常闲聊时已经说得够多了。
但现在蛇鲨近在咫尺，我必须重申一遍！
捕猎它是你们无上光荣的使命！

"设下陷阱，不停寻找
千百努力，不停找寻，
高举猎叉，满怀希望，

据其痕迹，索其性命。

"蛇鲨是罕见稀有的生物，
常规方法难将其捕获。
所有你们了解、不了解的方法都要用上：
不放过任何能够捕猎到它的机会！

"带着每一个英格兰人的期望——我负重前行。
这句格言极具激励性，但是太过老生常谈。
你们最好取出包里所有在猎捕打斗的过程中
能够护身的东西来武装自己。"

班克填了一张空白支票
（一张他签过字的支票）
并将一些散银兑换成票据。
贝克细心梳了梳自己的胡须和头发，
掸掉外罩上的灰尘。

布茨和布洛克轮流在一个磨刀石上埋头苦干——
磨一把铁锹。
只有海狸继续做着蕾丝花边，

对于大家所关切之事毫无兴趣。

律师抗议海狸的傲慢，
举例力证
做蕾丝花边侵犯了劳动权益
但这种申诉毫无功效。

班纳特的造物主残忍策划，
他的命运危机四伏。
而上帝对比拉德非常仁慈
只是在他样貌上多了点小差错。

屠夫变得很紧张，
穿戴整齐，正式威严，
黄色的羔皮手套、白色的轮状皱领——
说感觉自己就像是要去参加一场晚宴，
贝尔曼宣布的"丰盛晚宴"。

"告诉你们吧，那里有个好家伙，"他说道，
"如果我们有幸能够碰到它的话！"
这个时候，贝尔曼明智地点了点头，

说道:"这个完全取决于天气。"

这个时候,海狸笨拙地、慢悠悠地走过,
看到了屠夫,还是如此的惊恐。
即便是愚蠢而且笨拙的贝克,
也对贝尔曼的话表现出了极大的赞同。

"像个男人一样!"听到屠夫的啜泣声,
贝尔曼愤怒地说道。
"说不定我们会遇到毛毛,那个让人极度渴望的鸟,
打起十二万分的精神来完成这项挑战吧!"

第五幕

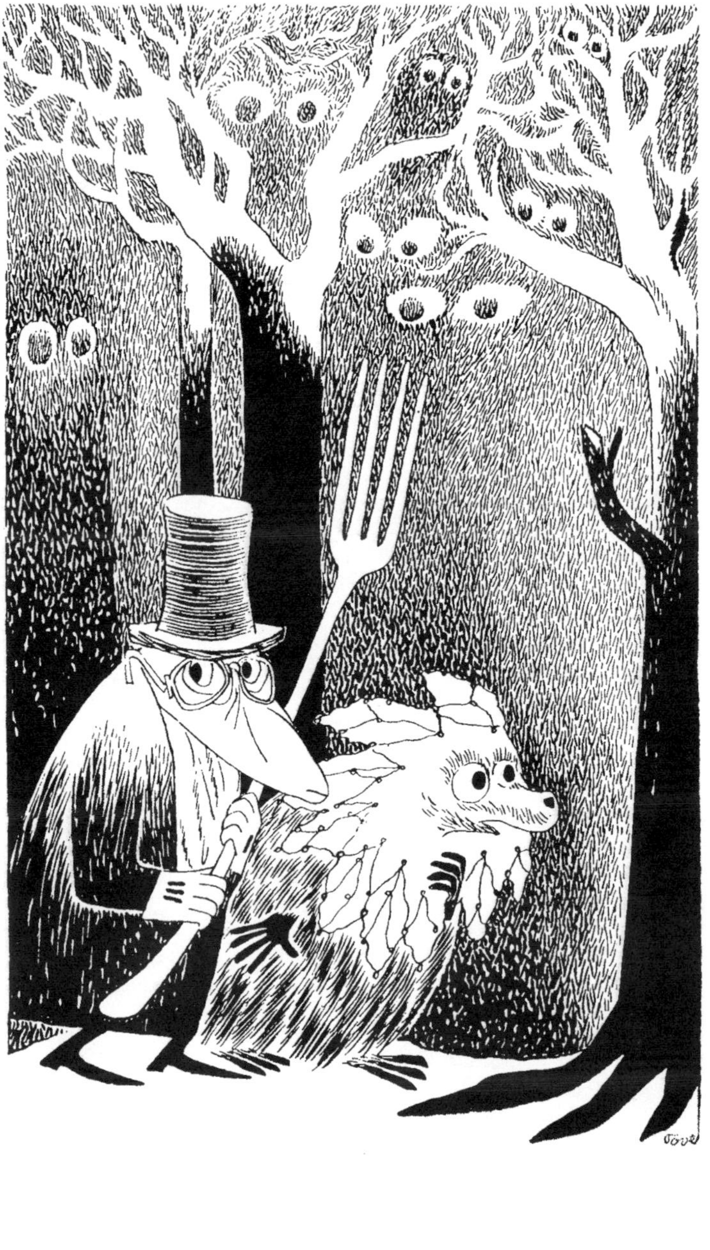

海狸的教训

设下陷阱,不停寻找
千百努力,不停找寻,
高举猎叉,满怀希望,
据其痕迹,索其性命。

屠夫独创计划,
私自出击;
将目的地锁定在一个
人迹罕至、凄凉孤寂的山谷。

海狸计划又重复,
锁定相同的猎场:
但由于未做记号和标识,
所以总是
徒劳无功,心生厌恶。

所有人都在想着"蛇鲨"
以及捕获它时的荣耀;
每一个人,假装自己毫不在意

但对彼此的想法，心知肚明。

山谷变得越来越狭窄，
夜晚日渐黑暗和冰冷，
他们肩并着肩，继续前行。
（这不是因为紧张，也并非出于友好。）

一声嘶鸣——尖锐高亢，响彻天际，
危险正在悄悄降临。
海狸被恫吓，尾巴尖惨白，
屠夫也晕眩不已。

他想起童年，那久远的记忆——
想起那喜悦、烂漫的小时光——
此前的巨响，唤醒他脑海里残存的
那种铅笔在石板上划过的声音！

"这就是毛毛的声音！"他突然大喊道。
（他们总是称之为"傻瓜"的这个男人喊道。）
"正如贝尔曼曾经所讲，"他满心自豪地说道，
"我以前也曾经说过。"

"这就是毛毛的叫声,拜托你们想一想;
我已经说过两遍了。
"这个是毛毛之歌!证据已经很明显,
我现在说第三次。"

海狸一丝不苟地数着,
专注着每一个词:
但是当它第三遍开始重复时,
失去了信心和勇气,
在万分绝望中暴怒。

虽然会感觉痛苦,
一直没有数清楚,
但现在唯一能做的是,
敲敲它笨拙的脑袋,
能帮它数清楚。

"2加1——如果能这么数的话,"
它说着比画道,"用一个手指和拇指!"
满含泪水的回忆起来,早些年,

它做这些事情完全不费力气。

"这件事可以完成,"屠夫说道,"我想。
一定可以完成,我敢保证。
也将要被完成!给我拿纸和墨水,
现在最需要做的就是分秒必争,跟时间赛跑。"

海狸从丰富的物资中
拿出纸张、文件夹、钢笔和墨水;
用一双充满惊奇的眼睛注视着,
这些奇怪的、令人毛骨悚然的"生物"
从洞穴中倾巢而出。

屠夫异常专注,把东西铺开来,
然后每只手各握一支钢笔,
用简单普世、海狸能够理解的方式
解释着眼前的一切。

"既然我们已经得到'3'——
那之后的数字就好办了——
我们加到7,加到10,

直到1000，再减去8。

"结果非常明显，992
然后再减去17，之后的答案
必定是准确无疑的。"

"我很乐意解释一下自己的算法，
因为我的脑海里思路清晰，
如果我时间充裕，而你又聪明
那我们就有得聊了。

"迄今为止我们所经历的一切
都被一种神秘的气息包围着，
我费那么大的力气给你讲一堂博物学的课
都不用收取你费用。"

他以一种亲切的方式进行下去的时候说
（如果万事无规矩，
只有指令，没有说明，
那社会将，
天翻地覆）

毛毛这种被极度渴望的鸟，
永远满怀激情：
但是它的穿衣品位简直可笑——
与时尚毫不沾边。

这种鸟一旦遇到同类
也不会表现出友好。
只会在巢边礼貌性地问好，
只会一味索取而不施予善意。

它的香味，一言难尽
远远要比羊肉、牡蛎和鸡蛋这些食物
更加的香气四溢。
（有人说最好把它放在象牙罐子里，
有人说应该将它放在桃花心木的桶里。）

"用柴禾煮熟，外表涂上洋槐蜜，
然后用保鲜膜裹严实。
但是有一点非常重要——
就是在腌渍过程中保持它的形状。"

屠夫滔滔不绝，很乐意讲到明天，
但他知道"授课"必须马上结束，
喜极而泣地试图说明
他把海狸看做是自己的朋友。

海狸一副供认不讳、欣然接受的表情——
那意味深长的表情比泪水更让人动容，
十分钟之内所学到的
比过去七十年在书本中学到的都多。

然后，他们手拉着手往回走，贝尔曼，
（有那么片刻）带着惯有的严肃权威的表情，
说道："我们在这惊涛巨浪的大海上度过的每一天，
都是收获颇丰的！"

比如说海狸和屠夫，
他们素昧平生，现在情谊深厚；
冬去春来——
他们已经形影不离了。
大伙时常会发现，他们俩还是会争吵——

当争吵发生的时候，任何的努力都是徒劳。毛毛之歌总是在他们的脑海中不断地回响，而且永远巩固着他们的友情！

第六幕

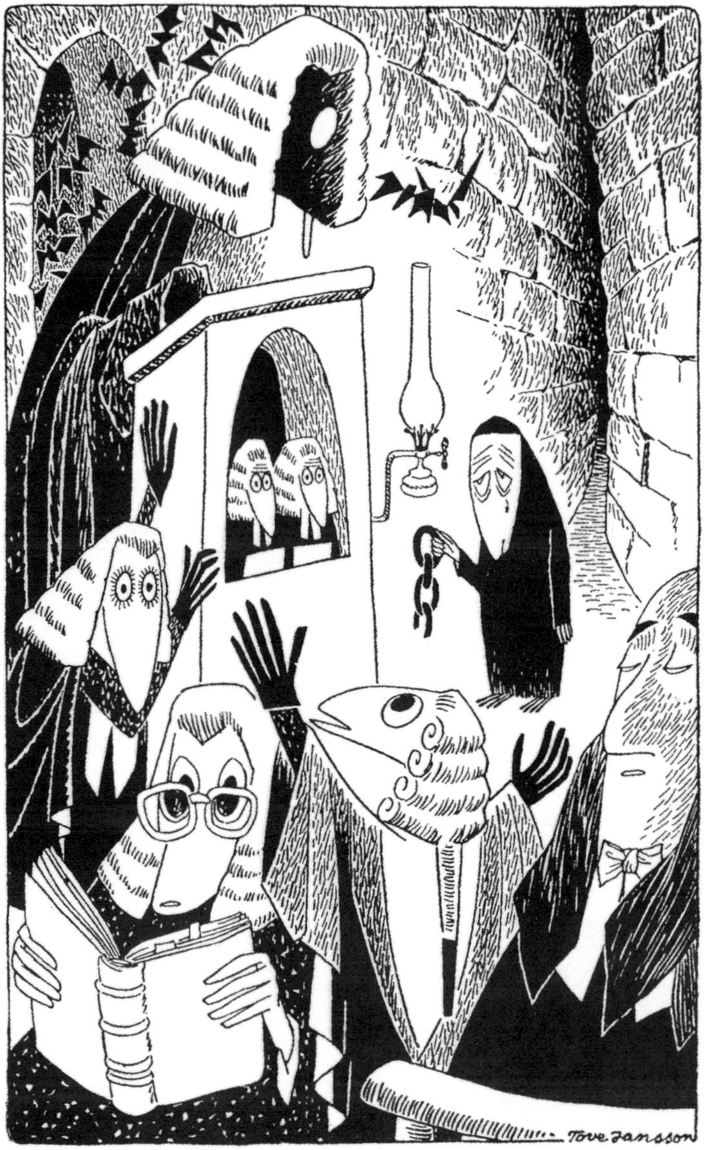
Tove Jansson

律师的梦想

设下陷阱,不停寻找
千百努力,不停找寻,
高举猎叉,满怀希望,
据其痕迹,索其性命。

但是律师,厌倦了徒劳的证实
海狸绣蕾丝是不当的行为,
入睡后,他在梦中异常清晰地看到了那种生物
他已经幻想了很久的生物。

他梦到自己站在朦胧虚无的法庭上,
在那儿,他看到戴着眼镜,
穿着长袍、戴着假发的蛇鲨,正在为一只
被控告逃离了猪圈的猪而辩护。

目击者证实,指控准确无疑,
猪圈被发现时就已空空如也:
法官用一种轻柔低沉的声音
阐述着法律的评判标准。

起诉书上从未清晰地表述过，
但是蛇鲨已经开始讲话了，
三个小时过去，还没有任何人猜出
到底这只猪之前做了什么。

（早在起诉书被宣读以前）
陪审团的人就各持己见，
七嘴八舌地同时议论起来，
以至于大家都不知道对方都讲了些什么。

"你必须知道——"法官刚要讲话，
却被蛇鲨厉声制止道："你胡说！"
现在的法律法规是如此的陈旧过时！
告诉你吧，我的朋友，所有的质疑都取决于
一个过时的归属权的问题。

"说到不忠（叛国罪），
我们应该帮助这只猪，而不是重判它：
就比如辩护词上写的是'从未负债'
那你凭什么控告它破产呢？"

"我不会为它逃亡的事实而争辩；
但是它的罪过，我相信，已经洗刷了
（目前为止牵扯到这个案子的诉讼成本）
因为那些不在场证据。

"我可怜的委托人的命运
取决于你们的投票。"
讲完落座，
呈上陈述笔记
简明扼要的结案陈词。

但是法官说他之前从来没有结案陈词过；
所以蛇鲨取而代之，
概括总结得如此之好，
比目击者的证言都要坚实有力！

判决时刻，陪审团拒绝给出意见，
判决书上的内容同样令人费解；
但是他们抱着侥幸的心理希望蛇鲨不会介意
继续承担辩护律师的职责。

经过一天异常辛苦的工作
蛇鲨发现，判决结果并未产生变化。
法庭最终判决"有罪！"，
陪审团陷入呻吟、抱怨，
一些人甚至昏厥。

蛇鲨宣读判决陈词，陪审团陷入一片寂静
大家都紧张得说不出一句话：
蛇鲨以及全体人员起立，之后的法庭陷入夜一般的静寂，
静到仿佛一根针坠落的声音都能被听到。

法庭的最终判决原本是"终身流放"，
然后改为"罚款40英镑"。
法官一再担心自己的陈词听起来会不合法。
但是陪审团的全体成员还是欢呼雀跃起来。

然而，狂欢随即戛然而止
因为一个狱卒满含泪水上前说，
这样的判决不会有任何作用了，
因为这只猪已经死了很多年了。

法官离开了,看起来沉重又沮丧。
但是蛇鲨,尽管也被惊吓到,
作为律师,据理力争到最后一刻
辩词也非常可信。

当贝尔曼拿着闹铃
用喧闹刺耳的铃声将他叫醒,
律师还在继续着他的梦,
梦中的哀号声也仿佛每时每刻都变得更加的清晰。

第七幕

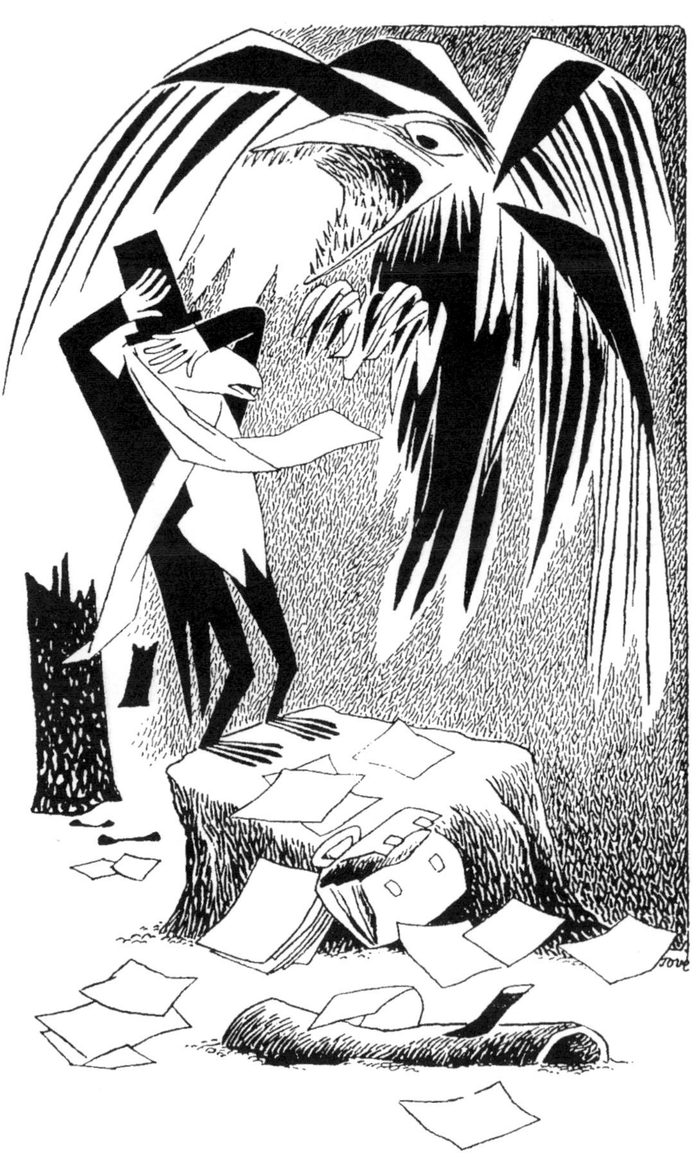

班克的命运

设下陷阱，不停寻找
千百努力，不停找寻，
高举猎叉，满怀希望，
据其痕迹，索其性命。

班克，跃跃欲试
简要来说，
就捕猎蛇鲨而言
他总是首当其冲
但又总是徒有满腔热情

他用套管仔细地搜捕蛇鲨时，
一只猛兽迅疾而悄然地接近
班克被擒，发出绝望的惨叫，
深知试图逃跑也是徒劳。

班克企图用钱贿赂怪兽——
拿出一张七磅十美分的抬头待写的支票

然而怪兽并不买账,
伸长脖子
再次擒住班克。

怪兽没有作片刻停顿——用它那尖利的爪子
开始野蛮残忍撕咬班克——
班克的身体在它的撕咬下不停晃动
他挣扎着,抗争着
直到最后筋疲力尽,晕倒在地上。

其他人闻风赶来,
猛兽展翅飞去:
贝尔曼说道:"这正是我最怕的!"
然后庄重地响铃。

班克的脸乌黑发青,
他们几乎都无法想起
那只怪兽大概的样子:
班克是如此深陷恐惧
以至于背心都已经被汗湿了——
"美好"的身材一览无余!

当天在场的所有人都被惊到。
他穿上自己整套的晚礼服,
表情痛苦地努力想讲出一些
自己已经无法再表达的东西。

当他坐下来以后——双手挠头——
用最古板的声音吟唱
然而,吟唱空虚无物,
伴随着身体发出的咯咯的颤抖声。
这一切都证实——他已精神错乱。

"留他在这里面对他的命运吧——已经太迟了!"
贝尔曼在惊恐之中大声喊道。
"我们已经浪费了大半天的时间,再浪费下去的话,
天黑之前我们是不可能抓得到蛇鲨的!"

第八幕

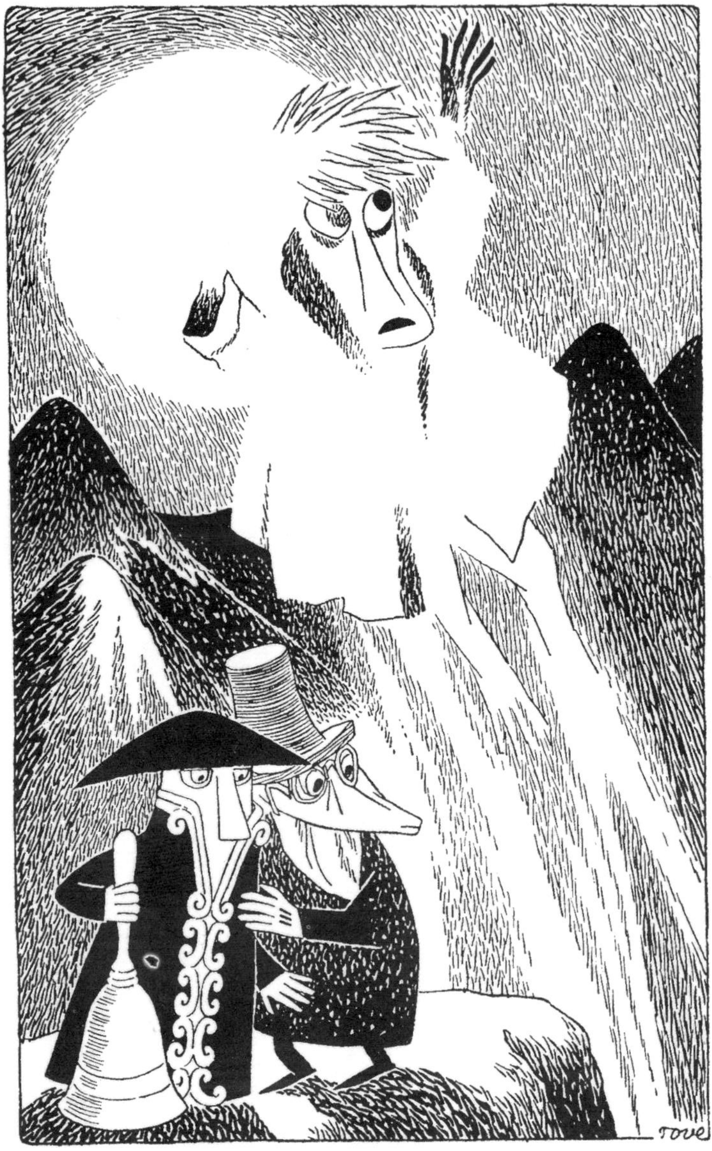
Tove

消失

设下陷阱,不停寻找
千百努力,不停找寻,
高举猎叉,满怀希望,
据其痕迹,索其性命。

他们惊恐之至,瑟瑟发抖中禁不住想此次追捕的失败,
海狸,最后兴奋异常,
一圈圈地追着自己的尾巴,
直到天色暗下来。

"这是多么具有警示意义的叫喊!"贝尔曼说道,
"它的叫喊声多么的疯狂,你们听听!
他挥动双手,摇头晃脑的样子,
必定是已经发现了蛇鲨!"

大家都兴奋地注视着彼此,
只有屠夫说道:
"他一直都是喜欢这么不顾一切地疯狂叫喊!"
他们观察着他——他们的贝克——他们的无名英雄——

在旁边的悬崖顶端站着。

有那么一刻,他看起来笔直而神圣,
紧接着,一个类似野人的轮廓
(好像痉挛发作)纵身跳入了峡谷,
大伙儿怀着敬畏的心情倾听、等待着。

"是蛇鲨!"他们第一次听到这样的叫喊声,
这种幸福来得太猝不及防而显得不真实。
紧接着,一片唏嘘和庆贺声:
当然也有不同的意见,认为"这是Boo……"

随后,死一般的寂静。
空气中一些奇怪的声响
一声疲倦且散漫的叹息声
听起来就像是"–jun[①]"
但是之后被否认说
这声音只不过是轻轻吹过的微风而已。

他们一直捕猎,直至夜色将至,发现
站在当初贝克发现蛇鲨的地方

---

① 与上段中的"Boo"呼应,两者合词为"Boojum",中文意思为"可怕的怪物"。

连一颗纽扣、一片羽毛,或者一个标志都没发现。

在世界的中心他尝试着说,
在他的笑声和欢乐声中,
他就这样悄无声息地突然消失了——
因为蛇鲨就是怪兽,明白了吧。

LEWIS CARROLL

THE HUNTING OF THE SNARK

ILLUSTRATED BY TOVE JANSSON

PREFACE

If – and the thing is wildly possible – the charge of writing nonsense were ever brought against the author of this brief but instructive poem, it would be based, I feel convinced, on the line (in Fit the Second) *'Then the bowsprit got mixed with the rudder sometimes'*.

In view of this painful possibility, I will not (as I might) appeal indignantly to my other writings as a proof that I am incapable of such a deed: I will not (as I might) point to the strong moral purpose of this poem itself, to the arithmetical principles so cautiously inculcated in it, or to its noble teachings in Natural History – I will take the more prosaic course of simply explaining how it happened.

The Bellman, who was almost morbidly sensitive about appearances, used to have the bowsprit un-shipped once or twice a week to be revarnished, and it more than once happened, when the time came for replacing it, that no one on board could remember which end of the ship it belonged to. They knew it was not of the slightest use to appeal to the Bellman about it – he would only refer to his Naval Code, and read out in pathetic tones Admiralty Instructions which none of them had ever been able to understand – so it generally ended in its being fastened on, anyhow, across the rudder. The helmsman used to stand by with tears in his eyes; he knew it was all wrong, but alas! Rule 42 of the Code, 'No one shall speak to the Man at the Helm,' had been completed by the Bellman himself with the words 'and the Man at the Helm shall speak to no one'. So remonstrance was impossible, and no steering could be done till the next varnishing day. During these bewildering intervals the ship usually sailed backwards.

As this poem is to some extent connected with the lay of the Jabberwock, let me take this opportunity of answering a question that has often been asked me, how to pronounce 'slithy toves.' The 'i' in 'slithy' is long, as in 'writhe'; and 'toves' is pronounced so as to rhyme with 'groves'. Again, the first 'o' in 'borogoves' is pronounced like the 'o' in 'borrow.' I have heard people try to give it the sound of the 'o' in 'worry'. Such is Human Perversity.

This also seems a fitting occasion to notice the other hard works in that poem. Humpty-Dumpty's theory, of two meanings packed into one word like a portmanteau, seems to me the right explanation for all.

For instance, take the two words 'fuming' and 'furious'. Make up your mind that you will say both words, but leave it unsettled which you will say first. Now open your mouth and speak. If your thoughts incline ever so little towards 'fuming', you will say 'fuming-furious'; if they turn, by even a hair's breadth, towards 'furious', you will say 'furious-fuming'; but if you have the rarest of gifts, a perfectly balanced mind, you will say 'frumious'.

Supposing that, when Pistol uttered the well-known words *'Under which king, Bezonian? Speak or die!'*,

Justice Shallow had felt certain that it was either William or Richard, but had not been able to settle which, so that he could not possibly say either name before the other – can it be doubted that, rather than die, he would have gasped out 'Rilchiam!'

FIT THE FIRST

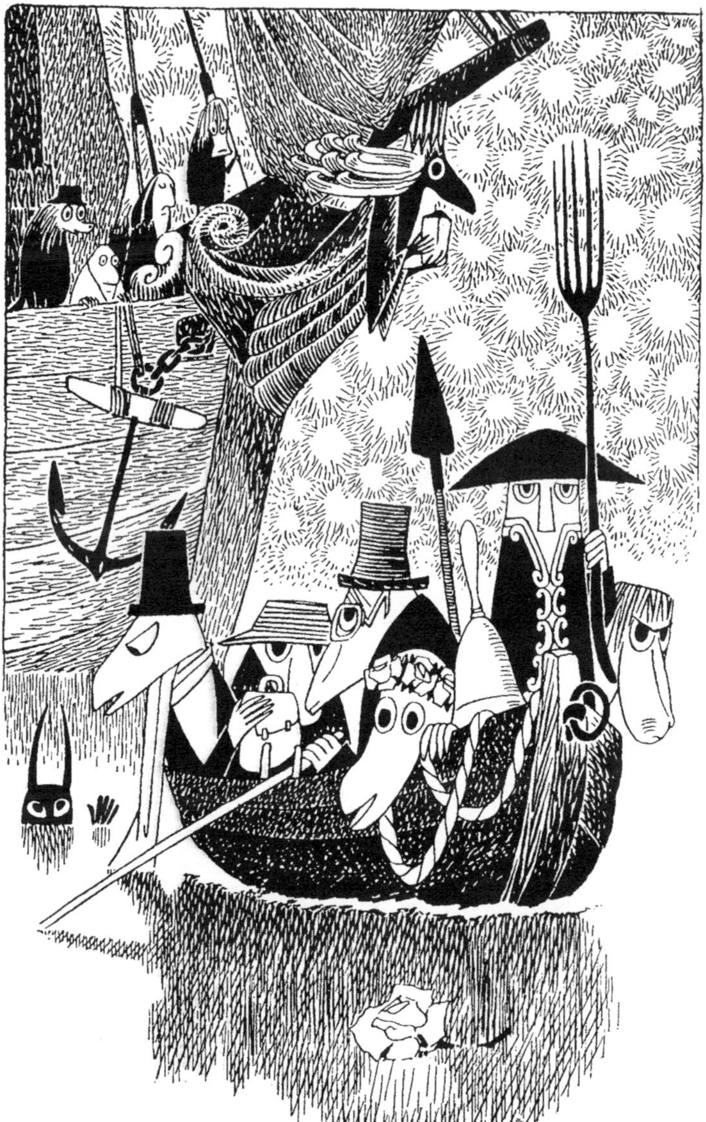
Tove

The Landing

'Just the place for a Snark!' the Bellman cried,
    As he landed his crew with care;
Supporting each man on the top of the tide
    By a finger entwined in his hair.

'Just the place for a Snark! I have said it twice:
    That alone should encourage the crew.
Just the place for a Snark! I have said it thrice:
    What I tell you three times is true.'

The crew was complete: it included a Boots –
    A maker of Bonnets and Hoods –
A Barrister, brought to arrange their disputes –
    And a Broker, to value their goods.

A Billiard-marker, whose skill was immense,
    Might perhaps have won more than his share –
But a Banker, engaged at enormous expense,
    Had the whole of their cash in his care.

There was also a Beaver, that paced on the deck,
    Or would sit making lace in the bow:
And had often (the Bellman said) saved them from wreck,
    Though none of the sailors knew how.

There was one who was famed for the number of things
    He forgot when he entered the ship:
His umbrella, his watch, all his jewels and rings
    And the clothes he had bought for the trip.

He had forty-two boxes, all carefully packed,
    With his name painted clearly on each:
But, since he omitted to mention the fact,
    They were all left behind on the beach.

The loss of his clothes hardly mattered, because
    He had seven coats on when he came,
With three pairs of boots – but the worst of it was,
    He had wholly forgotten his name.

He would answer to 'Hi!' or to any loud cry,
    Such as 'Fry me!' or 'Fritter my wig!'
To 'What-you-may-call-um!' or 'What-was-his-name!'
    But especially 'Thing-um-a-jig!'

While, for those who preferred a more forcible word,
    He had different names from these:
His intimate friends called him 'Candle-ends',
    And his enemies 'Toasted-cheese'.

'His form is ungainly – his intellect small –'
    (So the Bellman would often remark)
'But his courage is perfect! And that, after all,
    Is the thing that one needs with a Snark.'

He would joke with hyenas, returning their stare
  With an impudent wag of the head:
And he once went a walk, paw-in-paw, with a bear,
  'Just to keep up its spirits', he said.

He came as a Baker: but owned, when too late –
  And it drove the poor Bellman half-mad –
He could only bake Bridecake – for which, I may state,
  No materials were to be had.

The last of the crew needs especial remark,
  Though he looked an incredible dunce:
He had just one idea – but, that one being 'Snark',
  The good Bellman engaged him at once.

He came as a Butcher: but gravely declared,
  When the ship had been sailing a week,
He could only kill Beavers. The Bellman looked scared,
  And was almost too frightened to speak:

But at length he explained, in a tremulous tone,
  There was only one Beaver on board;
And that was a tame one he had of his own,
  Whose death would be deeply deplored.

The Beaver, who happened to hear the remark,
  Protested, with tears in its eyes,
That not even the rapture of hunting the Snark
  Could atone for that dismal surprise!

It strongly advised that the Butcher should be
    Conveyed in a separate ship:
But the Bellman declared that would never agree
    With the plans he had made for the trip:

Navigation was always a difficult art,
    Though with only one ship and one bell:
And he feared he must really decline, for his part,
    Undertaking another as well.

The Beaver's best course was, no doubt, to procure
    A second-hand dagger-proof coat –
So the Baker advised it – and next, to insure
    Its life in some Office of note:

This the Banker suggested, and offered for hire
    (On moderate terms), or for sale,
Two excellent Policies, one Against Fire,
    And one Against Damage From Hail.

Yet still, ever after that sorrowful day,
    Whenever the Butcher was by,
The Beaver kept looking the opposite way,
    And appeared unaccountably shy.

FIT THE SECOND

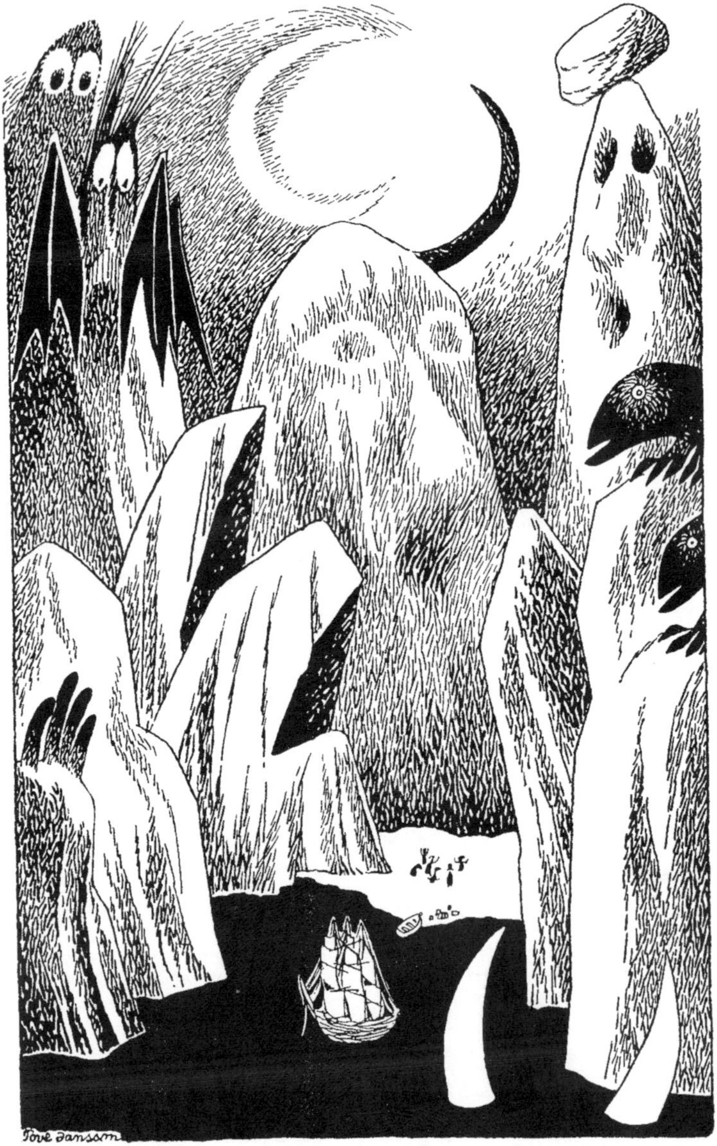
Tove Jansson

The Bellman's Speech

The Bellman himself they all praised to the skies –
    Such a carriage, such ease and such grace!
Such solemnity, too! One could see he was wise,
    The moment one looked in his face!

He had bought a large map representing the sea,
    Without the least vestige of land:
And the crew were much pleased when they found it to be
    A map they could all understand.

'What's the good of Mercator's North Poles and Equators,
    Tropics, Zones, and Meridian Lines?'
So the Bellman would cry: and the crew would reply
    'They are merely conventional signs!'

'Other maps are such shapes, with their islands and capes!
    But we've got our brave Captain to thank'
(So the crew would protest) 'that he's bought us the best –
    A perfect and absolute blank!'

This was charming, no doubt; but they shortly found out
    That the Captain they trusted so well
Had only one notion for crossing the ocean,
    And that was to tingle his bell.

He was thoughtful and grave – but the orders he gave
    Were enough to bewilder a crew.
When he cried 'Steer to starboard, but keep her head larboard!'
    What on earth was the helmsman to do?

Then the bowspit got mixed with the rudder sometimes:
    A thing, as the Bellman remarked,
That frequently happens in tropical climes,
    When a vessel is, so to speak, 'snarked'.

But the principal failing occurred in the sailing,
    And the Bellman, perplexed and distressed,
Said he *had* hoped, at least, when the wind blew due East,
    That the ship would *not* travel due West!

But the danger was past – they had landed at last,
    With their boxes, portmanteaus, and bags:
Yet at first sight the crew were not pleased with the view,
    Which consisted of chasms and crags.

The Bellman perceived that their spirits were low,
    And repeated in musical tone
Some jokes he had kept for a season of woe –
    But the crew would do nothing but groan.

He served out some grog with a liberal hand,
    And bade them sit down on the beach:
And they could not but own that their Captain looked grand,
    As he stood and delivered his speech.

'Friends, Romans, and countrymen, lend me your ears!'
     (They were all of them fond of quotations:
So they drank to his health, and they gave him three cheers,
     While he served out additional rations).

'We have sailed many months, we have sailed many weeks,
     (Four weeks to the month you may mark),
But never as yet ('tis your Captain who speaks)
     Have we caught the least glimpse of a Snark!

'We have sailed many weeks, we have sailed many days,
     (Seven days to the week I allow),
But a Snark, on the which we might lovingly gaze,
     We have never beheld till now!'

'Come, listen, my men, while I tell you again
     The five unmistakable marks
By which you may know, wheresoever you go,
     The warranted genuine Snarks.

'Let us take them in order. The first is the taste,
     Which is meager and hollow, but crisp:
Like a coat that is rather too tight in the waist,
     With a flavor of Will-o'-the-wisp.

'Its habit of getting up late you'll agree
     That it carries too far, when I say
That it frequently breakfasts at five-o'clock tea,
     And dines on the following day.

'The third is its slowness in taking a jest.
      Should you happen to venture on one,
It will sigh like a thing that is deeply distressed:
      And it always looks grave at a pun.

'The fourth is its fondness for bathing-machines,
      Which it constantly carries about,
And believes that they add to the beauty of scenes –
      A sentiment open to doubt.

'The fifth is ambition. It next will be right
      To describe each particular batch:
Distinguishing those that have feathers, and bite,
      And those that have whiskers, and scratch.

'For, although common Snarks do no manner of harm,
      Yet, I feel it my duty to say,
Some are Boojums –' The Bellman broke off in alarm,
      For the Baker had fainted away.

FIT THE THIRD

Tove Jansson

The Baker's Tale

They roused him with muffins – they roused him with ice –
    They roused him with mustard and cress –
They roused him with jam and judicious advice –
    They set him conundrums to guess.

When at length he sat up and was able to speak,
    His sad story he offered to tell;
And the Bellman cried 'Silence! Not even a shriek!'
    And excitedly tingled his bell.

There was silence supreme! Not a shriek, not a scream,
    Scarcely even a howl or a groan,
As the man they called 'Ho!' told his story of woe
    In an antediluvian tone.

'My father and mother were honest, though poor –'
    'Skip all that!' cried the Bellman in haste.
'If it once becomes dark, there's no chance of a Snark –
    We have hardly a minute to waste!'

'I skip forty years,' said the Baker, in tears,
    'And proceed without further remark
To the day when you took me aboard of your ship
    To help you in hunting the Snark.

'A dear uncle of mine (after whom I was named)
    Remarked, when I bade him farewell –'
'Oh, skip your dear uncle!' the Bellman exclaimed,
    As he angrily tingled his bell.

'He remarked to me then,' said that mildest of men,
    '"If your Snark be a Snark, that is right:
Fetch it home by all means – you may serve it with greens,
    And it's handy for striking a light.

'"You may seek it with thimbles – and seek it with care;
    You may hunt it with forks and hope;
    You may threaten its life with a railway-share;
    You may charm it with smiles and soap –"'

('That's exactly the method,' the Bellman bold
    In a hasty parenthesis cried,
'That's exactly the way I have always been told
    That the capture of Snarks should be tried!')

'"But oh, beamish nephew, beware of the day,
    If your Snark be a Boojum! For then
You will softly and suddenly vanish away,
    And never be met with again!'

'It is this, it is this that oppresses my soul,
    When I think of my uncle's last words:
And my heart is like nothing so much as a bowl

'It is this, it is this –' 'We have had that before!'
    The Bellman indignantly said.
And the Baker replied 'Let me say it once more.
    It is this, it is this that I dread!

'I engage with the Snark – every night after dark –
    In a dreamy delirious fight:
I serve it with greens in those shadowy scenes,
    And I use it for striking a light:

'But if ever I meet with a Boojum, that day,
    In a moment (of this I am sure),
I shall softly and suddenly vanish away –
    And the notion I cannot endure!'

FIT THE FOURTH

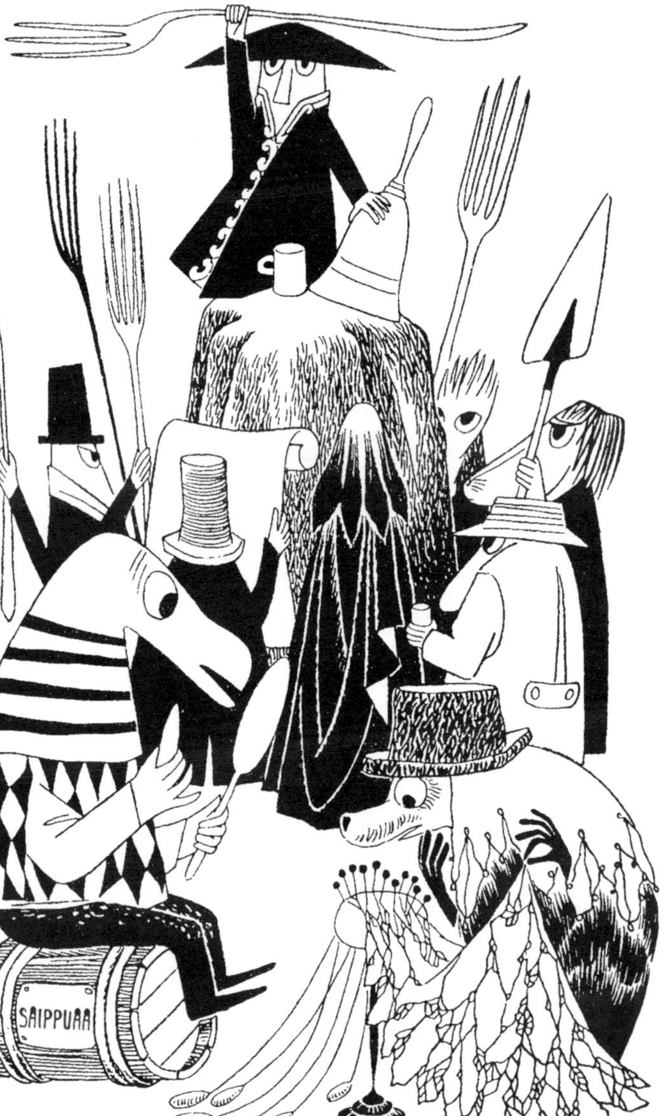
SAIPPUAA
Tove

The Hunting

The Bellman looked uffish, and wrinkled his brow.
    'If only you'd spoken before!
It's excessively awkward to mention it now,
    With the Snark, so to speak, at the door!

'We should all of us grieve, as you well may believe,
    If you never were met with again –
But surely, my man, when the voyage began,
    You might have suggested it then?

'It's excessively awkward to mention it now –
    As I think I've already remarked.'
And the man they called 'Hi!' replied, with a sigh,
    'I informed you the day we embarked.

'You may charge me with murder – or want of sense –
    (We are all of us weak at times):
But the slightest approach to a false pretence
    Was never among my crimes!

'I said it in Hebrew – I said it in Dutch –
    I said it in German and Greek:
But I wholly forgot (and it vexes me much)
    That English is what you speak!'

"'Tis a pitiful tale,' said the Bellman, whose face
      Had grown longer at every word:
'But, now that you've stated the whole of your case,
      More debate would be simply absurd.

'The rest of my speech' (he explained to his men)
      'You shall hear when I've leisure to speak it.
But the Snark is at hand, let me tell you again!
      'Tis your glorious duty to seek it!

'To seek it with thimbles, to seek it with care;
      To pursue it with forks and hope;
To threaten its life with a railway-share;
      To charm it with smiles and soap!

'For the Snark's a peculiar creature, that won't
      Be caught in a commonplace way.
Do all that you know, and try all that you don't:
      Not a chance must be wasted to-day!

'For England expects – I forbear to proceed:
      'Tis a maxim tremendous, but trite:
And you'd best be unpacking the things that you need
      To rig yourselves out for the fight.'

Then the Banker endorsed a blank cheque (which he crossed),
      And changed his loose silver for notes.
The Baker with care combed his whiskers and hair,
      And shook the dust out of his coats.

The Boots and the Broker were sharpening a spade –
    Each working the grindstone in turn:
But the Beaver went on making lace, and displayed
    No interest in the concern:

Though the Barrister tried to appeal to its pride,
    And vainly proceeded to cite
A number of cases, in which making laces
    Had been proved an infringement of right.

The maker of Bonnets ferociously planned
    A novel arrangement of bows:
While the Billiard-marker with quivering hand
    Was chalking the tip of his nose.

But the Butcher turned nervous, and dressed himself fine,
    With yellow kid gloves and a ruff –
Said he felt it exactly like going to dine,
    Which the Bellman declared was all 'stuff'.

'Introduce me, now there's a good fellow,' he said,
    'If we happen to meet it together!'
And the Bellman, sagaciously nodding his head,
    Said 'That must depend on the weather.'

The Beaver went simply galumphing about,
    At seeing the Butcher so shy:
And even the Baker, though stupid and stout,
    Made an effort to wink with one eye.

'Be a man!' said the Bellman in wrath, as he heard
    The Butcher beginning to sob.
'Should we meet with a Jubjub, that desperate bird,
    We shall need all our strength for the job!'

FIT THE FIFTH

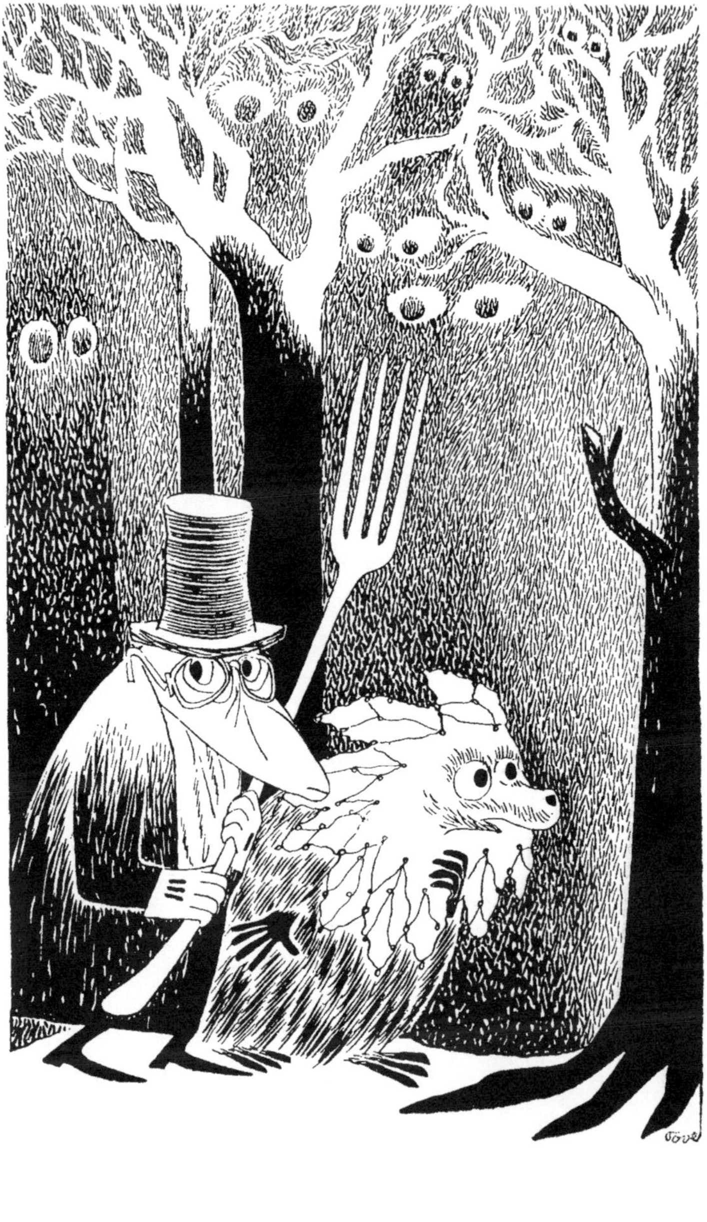

The Beaver's Lesson

They sought it with thimbles, they sought it with care;
    They pursued it with forks and hope;
They threatened its life with a railway-share;
    They charmed it with smiles and soap.

Then the Butcher contrived an ingenious plan
    For making a separate sally;
And fixed on a spot unfrequented by man,
    A dismal and desolate valley.

But the very same plan to the Beaver occurred:
    It had chosen the very same place:
Yet neither betrayed, by a sign or a word,
    The disgust that appeared in his face.

Each thought he was thinking of nothing but 'Snark'
    And the glorious work of the day;
And each tried to pretend that he did not remark
    That the other was going that way.

But the valley grew narrow and narrower still,
    And the evening got darker and colder,
Till (merely from nervousness, not from goodwill)
    They marched along shoulder to shoulder.

Then a scream, shrill and high, rent the shuddering sky,
    And they knew that some danger was near:
The Beaver turned pale to the tip of its tail,
    And even the Butcher felt queer.

He thought of his childhood, left far far behind –
    That blissful and innocent state –
The sound so exactly recalled to his mind
    A pencil that squeaks on a slate!

''Tis the voice of the Jubjub!' he suddenly cried.
    (This man, that they used to call 'Dunce'.)
'As the Bellman would tell you,' he added with pride,
    'I have uttered that sentiment once.

''Tis the note of the Jubjub! Keep count, I entreat;
    You will find I have told it you twice.
'Tis the song of the Jubjub! The proof is complete,
    If only I've stated it thrice'.

The Beaver had counted with scrupulous care,
    Attending to every word:
But it fairly lost heart, and outgrabe in despair,
    When the third repetition occurred.

It felt that, in spite of all possible pains,
    It had somehow contrived to lose count,
And the only thing now was to rack its poor brains
    By reckoning up the amount.

'Two added to one – if that could but be done,'
    It said, 'with one's fingers and thumbs!'
Recollecting with tears how, in earlier years,
    It had taken no pains with its sums.

'The thing can be done,' said the Butcher, 'I think.
    The thing must be done, I am sure.
The thing shall be done! Bring me paper and ink,
    The best there is time to procure.'

The Beaver brought paper, portfolio, pens,
    And ink in unfailing supplies:
While strange creepy creatures came out of their dens,
    And watched them with wondering eyes.

So engrossed was the Butcher, he heeded them not,
    As he wrote with a pen in each hand,
And explained all the while in a popular style
    Which the Beaver could well understand.

'Taking Three as the subject to reason about –
    A convenient number to state –
We add Seven, and Ten, and then multiply out
    By One Thousand diminished by Eight.

'The result we proceed to divide, as you see,
    By Nine Hundred and Ninety Two:
Then subtract Seventeen, and the answer must be
    Exactly and perfectly true.

'The method employed I would gladly explain,
          While I have it so clear in my head,
If I had but the time and you had but the brain –
          But much yet remains to be said.

'In one moment I've seen what has hitherto been
          Enveloped in absolute mystery,
And without extra charge I will give you at large
          A Lesson in Natural History.'

In his genial way he proceeded to say
          (Forgetting all laws of propriety,
And that giving instruction, without introduction,
          Would have caused quite a thrill in Society),

'As to temper the Jubjub's a desperate bird,
          Since it lives in perpetual passion:
Its taste in costume is entirely absurd –
          It is ages ahead of the fashion:

'But it knows any friend it has met once before:
          It never will look at a bride:
And in charity-meetings it stands at the door,
          And collects – though it does not subscribe.

'Its flavour when cooked is more exquisite far
          Than mutton, or oysters, or eggs:
(Some think it keeps best in an ivory jar,
          And some, in mahogany kegs:)

'You boil it in sawdust: you salt it in glue:
    You condense it with locusts and tape:
Still keeping one principal object in view –
    To preserve its symmetrical shape.'

The Butcher would gladly have talked till next day,
    But he felt that the lesson must end,
And he wept with delight in attempting to say
    He considered the Beaver his friend.

While the Beaver confessed, with affectionate looks
    More eloquent even than tears,
It had learned in ten minutes far more than all books
    Would have taught it in seventy years.

They returned hand-in-hand, and the Bellman, unmanned
    (For a moment) with noble emotion,
Said 'This amply repays all the wearisome days
    We have spent on the billowy ocean!'

Such friends, as the Beaver and Butcher became,
    Have seldom if ever been known;
In winter or summer, 'twas always the same –
    You could never meet either alone.

And when quarrels arose – as one frequently finds
    Quarrels will, spite of every endeavour –
The song of the Jubjub recurred to their minds,
    And cemented their friendship for ever!

FIT THE SIXTH

The Barrister's Dream

They sought it with thimbles, they sought it with care;
    They pursued it with forks and hope;
They threatened its life with a railway-share;
    They charmed it with smiles and soap.

But the Barrister, weary of proving in vain
    That the Beaver's lace-making was wrong,
Fell asleep, and in dreams saw the creature quite plain
    That his fancy had dwelt on so long.

He dreamed that he stood in a shadowy Court,
    Where the Snark, with a glass in its eye,
Dressed in gown, bands, and wig, was defending a pig
    On the charge of deserting its sty.

The Witnesses proved, without error or flaw,
    That the sty was deserted when found:
And the Judge kept explaining the state of the law
    In a soft under-current of sound.

The indictment had never been clearly expressed,
    And it seemed that the Snark had begun,
And had spoken three hours, before any one guessed
    What the pig was supposed to have done.

The Jury had each formed a different view
    (Long before the indictment was read),
And they all spoke at once, so that none of them knew
    One word that the others had said.

'You must know –' said the Judge: but the Snark exclaimed
    'Fudge!' That statute is obsolete quite!
Let me tell you, my friends, the whole question depends
    On an ancient manorial right.

'In the matter of Treason the pig would appear
    To have aided, but scarcely abetted:
While the charge of Insolvency fails, it is clear,
    If you grant the plea 'never indebted'.

'The fact of Desertion I will not dispute;
    But its guilt, as I trust, is removed
(So far as related to the costs of this suit)
    By the Alibi which has been proved.

'My poor client's fate now depends on your votes.'
    Here the speaker sat down in his place,
And directed the Judge to refer to his notes
    And briefly to sum up the case.

But the Judge said he never had summed up before;
    So the Snark undertook it instead,
And summed it so well that it came to far more
    Than the Witnesses ever had said!

When the verdict was called for, the Jury declined,
    As the word was so puzzling to spell;
But they ventured to hope that the Snark wouldn't mind
    Undertaking that duty as well.

So the Snark found the verdict, although, as it owned,
    It was spent with the toils of the day:
When it said the word 'GUILTY!' the Jury all groaned,
    And some of them fainted away.

Then the Snark pronounced sentence, the Judge being quite
    Too nervous to utter a word:
When it rose to its feet, there was silence like night,
    And the fall of a pin might be heard.

'Transportation for life' was the sentence it gave,
    'And *then* to be fined forty pound.'
The Jury all cheered, though the Judge said he feared
    That the phrase was not legally sound.

But their wild exultation was suddenly checked
    When the jailer informed them, with tears,
Such a sentence would have not the slightest effect,
    As the pig had been dead for some years.

The Judge left the Court, looking deeply disgusted:
    But the Snark, though a little aghast,
As the lawyer to whom the defense was entrusted,
    Went bellowing on to the last.

Thus the Barrister dreamed, while the bellowing seemed
    To grow every moment more clear:
Till he woke to the knell of a furious bell,
    Which the Bellman rang close at his ear.

FIT THE SEVENTH

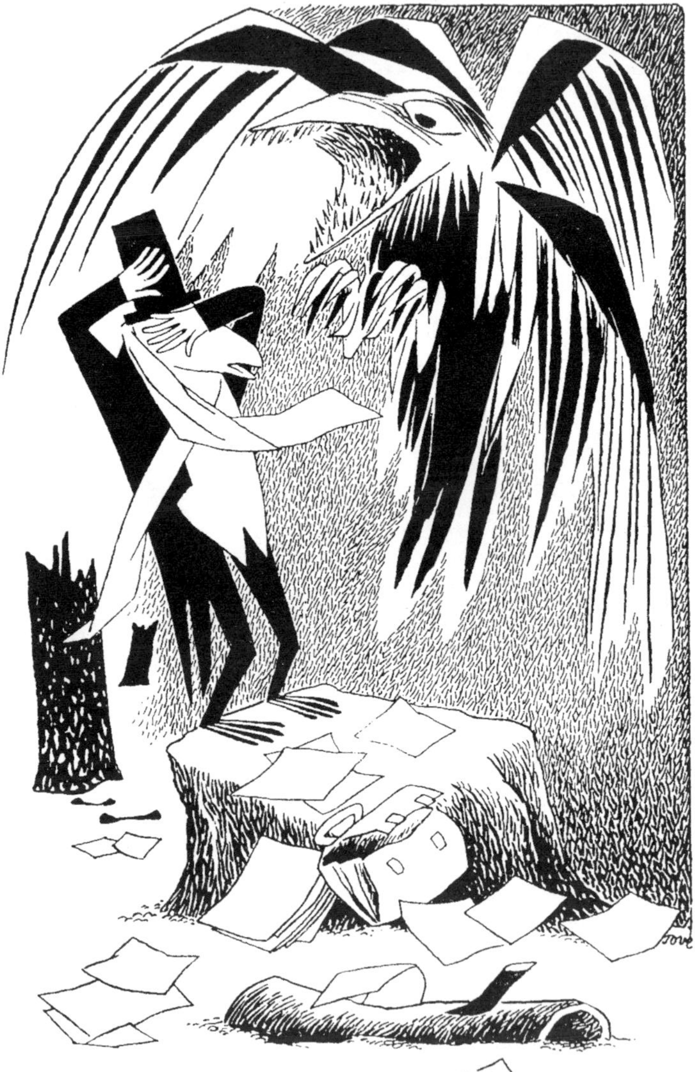

The Banker's Fate

They sought it with thimbles, they sought it with care;
    They pursued it with forks and hope;
They threatened its life with a railway-share;
    They charmed it with smiles and soap.

And the Banker, inspired with a courage so new
    It was matter for general remark,
Rushed madly ahead and was lost to their view
    In his zeal to discover the Snark

But while he was seeking with thimbles and care,
    A Bandersnatch swiftly drew nigh
And grabbed at the Banker, who shrieked in despair,
    For he knew it was useless to fly.

He offered large discount – he offered a cheque
    (Drawn 'to bearer') for seven-pounds-ten:
But the Bandersnatch merely extended its neck
    And grabbed at the Banker again.

Without rest or pause – while those frumious jaws
    Went savagely snapping around –
He skipped and he hopped, and he floundered and flopped,
    Till fainting he fell to the ground.

The Bandersnatch fled as the others appeared
    Led on by that fear-stricken yell:
And the Bellman remarked 'It is just as I feared!'
    And solemnly tolled on his bell.

He was black in the face, and they scarcely could trace
    The least likeness to what he had been:
While so great was his fright that his waistcoat turned
    A wonderful thing to be seen!

To the horror of all who were present that day.
    He uprose in full evening dress,
And with senseless grimaces endeavoured to say
    What his tongue could no longer express.

Down he sank in a chair – ran his hands through his hair
    And chanted in mimsiest tones
Words whose utter inanity proved his insanity,
    While he rattled a couple of bones.

'Leave him here to his fate – it is getting so late!'
    The Bellman exclaimed in a fright.
'We have lost half the day. Any further delay,
    And we shan't catch a Snark before night!'

FIT THE EIGHTH

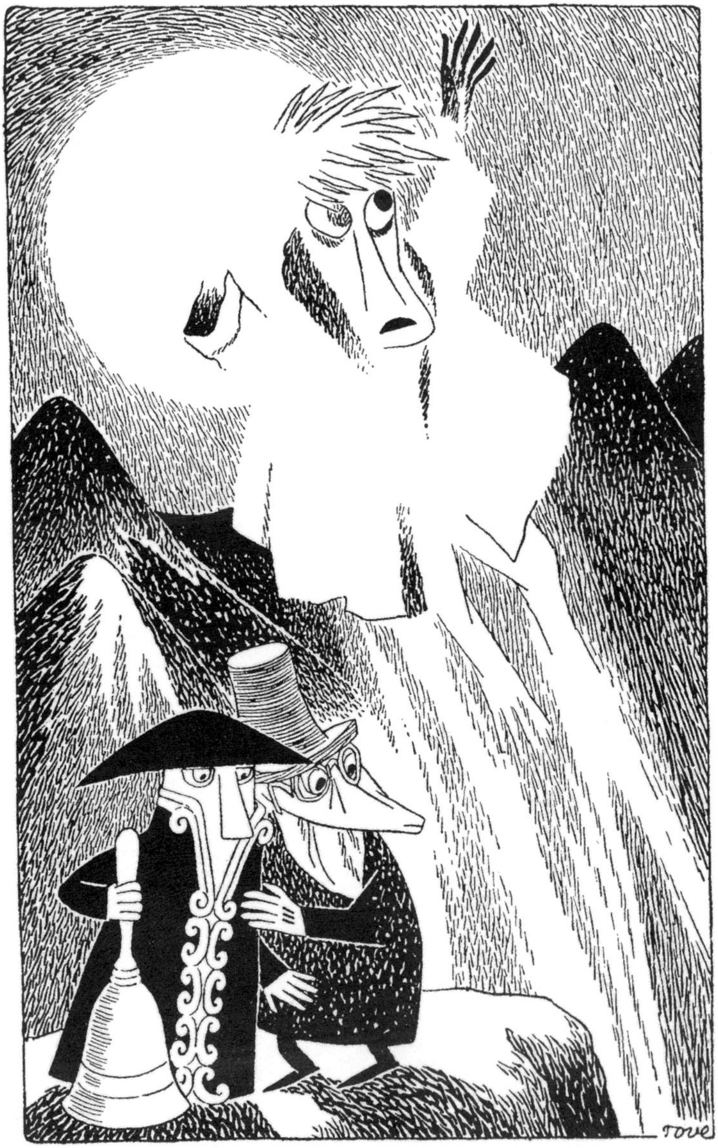
Tove

The Vanishing

They sought it with thimbles, they sought it with care;
    They pursued it with forks and hope;
They threatened its life with a railway-share;
    They charmed it with smiles and soap.

They shuddered to think that the chase might fail,
    And the Beaver, excited at last,
Went bounding along on the tip of its tail,
    For the daylight was nearly past.

'There is Thingumbob shouting!' the Bellman said,
    'He is shouting like mad, only hark!
He is waving his hands, he is wagging his head,
    He has certainly found a Snark!'

They gazed in delight, while the Butcher exclaimed
    'He was always a desperate wag!'
They beheld him – their Baker – their hero unnamed –
    On the top of a neighbouring crag.

Erect and sublime, for one moment of time.
    In the next, that wild figure they saw
(As if stung by a spasm) plunge into a chasm,
    While they waited and listened in awe.

'It's a Snark!' was the sound that first came to their ears,
    And seemed almost too good to be true.
Then followed a torrent of laughter and cheers:
    Then the ominous words 'It's a Boo-'

Then, silence. Some fancied they heard in the air
    A weary and wandering sigh
That sounded like '-jum!' but the others declare
    It was only a breeze that went by.

They hunted till darkness came on, but they found
    Not a button, or feather, or mark,
By which they could tell that they stood on the ground
    Where the Baker had met with the Snark.

In the midst of the word he was trying to say,
    In the midst of his laughter and glee,
He had softly and suddenly vanished away –
    For the Snark *was* a Boojum, you see.